_____ *landed*
(baby's name)

on _____
(date)

in _____
(place)

**To Aaron Morris, Helen Margaret and Carol Lenore
for being landed with me. — J.M.**

In loving memory of my mother, Frances Bronson. — L.B.

Book design by Kristen M. Nobles.
Typeset in Wilke Bold and Palatino.
The illustrations in this book were rendered in oil paint.
Printed in Hong Kong.

ISBN 0-8118-2674-0

Distributed in Canada by Raincoast Books
8680 Cambie Street, Vancouver, British Columbia V6P 6M9

10 9 8 7 6 5 4 3 2 1

Chronicle Books
85 Second Street, San Francisco, California 94105

www.chroniclebooks.com/Kids

The Babies Are Landing

by **Joan Margalith**

illustrated by **Linda Bronson**

chronicle books · san francisco

There are so many places to land on Earth
it all gets decided long before birth
Every baby's landing is carefully planned
at this very moment, in that very land

$\mathcal{A}$nd it's just as sure
     as the nose on your face
That each baby lands
     in exactly the right place

_T_his baby landed

on an island in the sea

$\mathcal{T}$hat baby landed
beneath a butterfly tree

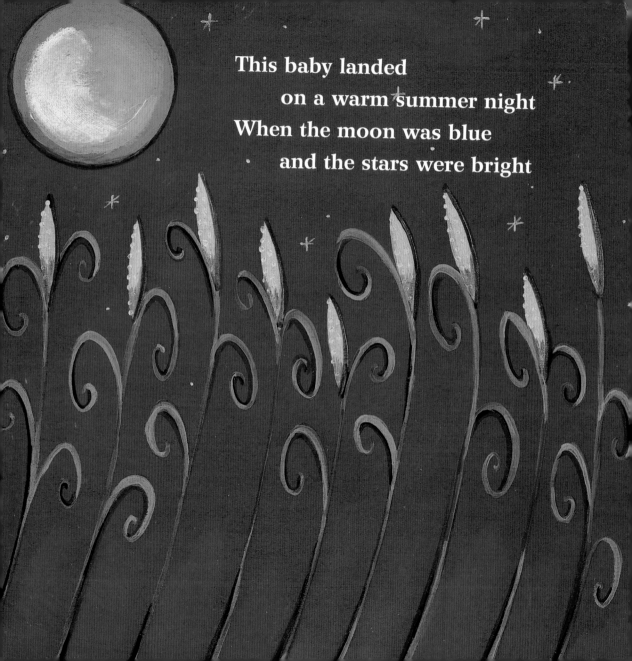

This baby landed
on a warm summer night
When the moon was blue
and the stars were bright

*T*his baby landed
   at the stroke of eleven
Look closely in her eyes
   and you might see heaven

$\mathscr{E}$very baby lands
in somebody's arms
In the roar of a city

or the hush of a farm

Some babies land solo
	and some land together
Side by side
	like birds of a feather

$\mathcal{W}$herever a baby lands
  he gets his very own name
And from that moment on
  the world will never be the same

*T*housands of babies land
on any given day
You've landed with us and
we wouldn't have it any other way

Look! Another baby is landing
Listen to the bells chime
Welcome to Earth, baby
You've landed at just the right time!